llama a

Anna Dewdney

doctors are here to help!

Based on the bestselling children's book series
by Anna Dewdney

A GOLDEN BOOK • NEW YORK

Copyright © Anna E. Dewdney Literary Trust.
Copyright © 2021 Genius Brands International, Inc.
Published in the United States by Golden Books, an
imprint of Random House Children's Books, a division
of Penguin Random House LLC, 1745 Broadway, New
York, NY 10019, and in Canada by Penguin Random
House Canada Limited, Toronto. Golden Books,
A Golden Book, A Little Golden Book, the
G colophon, and the distinctive gold spine are
registered trademarks of Penguin Random House LLC.

rhcbooks.com

Educators and librarians, for a variety of teaching tools,
visit us at RHTeachersLibrarians.com

ISBN 978-0-593-42645-6 (trade)
ISBN 978-0-593-42646-3 (ebook)

Printed in the United States of America
10 9 8 7 6 5 4 3 2 1

Llama Llama is playing on the swings with his friend Euclid. They are having so much fun!

"This time I'm going to swing really hard, and then jump far!" says Llama Llama.

Llama jumps off the swing just as Gilroy Goat jumps off the slide.

Oh, no—they crash! Poor Llama Llama gets a cut on his chin.

Their teacher, Zelda Zebra, comes out with her first-aid kit.

"You'll be fine, Llama Llama," she says, "although a doctor should take a look at you." She calls Mama Llama.

Later that day, Mama Llama makes an appointment for Llama Llama to see Dr. Hackney.
But Llama Llama does *not* want to go!

"I have Gilroy's ice cream party to go to," says Llama. "And my chin is absolutely, definitely okay."

Mama Llama can see that it still hurts him. She tells Llama that she used to be nervous about going to the doctor, too.

"But there was nothing to worry about," she says. "Doctors are here to help us."

Llama Llama's friends come over to see how he's feeling. He tells them he doesn't want to go to the doctor.

Luna says she was scared when she had to go to the eye doctor for the first time. "But the doctor was so nice!" she says.

Gilroy says when he goes to the doctor, he thinks about all the cool stuff that's going to happen after the visit. "Like my ice cream party. Think about that instead!" he tells Llama Llama.

"The actual doctor visit is never as bad as you imagine," says Euclid.

Llama Llama still doesn't want to go.

Then Hildy tells everyone that Dr. Hackney is her dad, and that he taught her a secret so she wouldn't be scared to get a checkup.

"I make up a mantra," she explains. "It's a thing or sound you say to yourself over and over to make you feel better." She says her mantra for everyone: "I'm a happy horsey hero."

Hildy helps Llama Llama make up his own mantra. "I'm a brave little llama," he says. It helps, but Llama is still a bit nervous.

When it's time to go to the doctor, Mama Llama looks all over for Llama Llama. She finds him hiding behind a chair.

"Please don't make me go, Mama," he begs. Mama Llama tells him she'll be with him the whole time.

Llama Llama decides to take along his stuffed animal, Fuzzy.

On the way to the doctor's office, Llama Llama tells Mama why he's scared.

"He might not be nice, or he'll do something that hurts, or he'll say I have to come back more," says Llama Llama.

Mama Llama reminds him that the doctor wants to help him, just like the doctor helped his friends.

In the waiting room at the doctor's office, Llama says his mantra a few times: "I'm a brave little llama." He also holds Fuzzy and thinks about all the ice cream he's going to eat at Gilroy's party later. Soon the nurse calls his name.

Llama Llama and Mama Llama go into an exam room. When Dr. Hackney comes in, he is really nice.

"When I was a kid, I never liked going to the doctor, either," he tells Llama. "One time, I even hid behind the couch!"

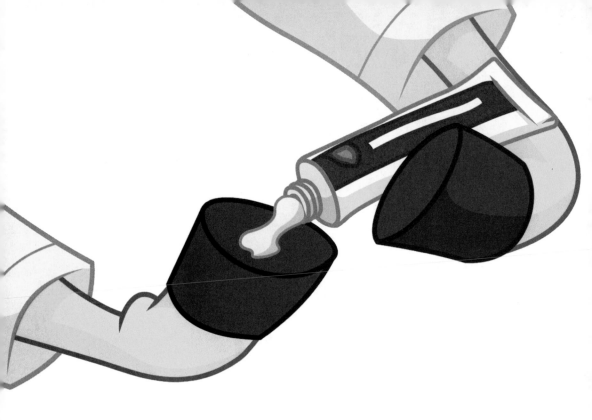

Then Dr. Hackney looks at Llama's chin. He gently puts a dab of cream and a new bandage on it and tells Llama Llama it will be better in a few days.

"That's it?" asks Llama Llama. "No shot? No stitches? Not even a checkup?"

"If you really want a checkup, why don't you do a checkup on me?" says Dr. Hackney. He gives Llama Llama his stethoscope.

Llama Llama listens to the doctor's heart. Then he checks his throat, his ears, and his knees.

Going to the doctor is fun!

On the way out, Llama meets a nervous hedgehog in the waiting room.

"Was the doctor really scary?" asks the hedgehog.

"No, he was great. Doctors are here to help you," says Llama Llama. Then he tells the hedgehog all the things that helped him feel better about his visit. The hedgehog starts to feel better, too!

"Llama Llama,
I am so proud of
you," says
Mama Llama.

Later, Mama Llama takes Llama to Gilroy's house for the ice cream party. He tells his friends about his doctor appointment.

"I did everything you said, and it worked!" says Llama.

"Thanks for being the best friends a llama could have," Llama says. "I couldn't have faced my fears without you."

"Llama, now that you're all patched up, what do you want to do?" asks Euclid.

"If it's okay with Gilroy," says Llama, "I think it's time for ice cream!"

"Yay!" the friends cheer.